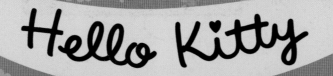
Hello Kitty

I Love My Mummy

HarperCollins *Children's Books*

Hello Kitty thinks
her mummy is the
greatest ever.

She's simply the best at giving hugs!

Hello Kitty knows her mummy works very hard...

but she still
has time to play!

Mummy and Hello Kitty
love to go for walks,
even when it's raining.

Splashing through the puddles is so much fun!

When Hello Kitty is frightened,
Mummy is always there...

to make her feel safe and secure.

Hello Kitty and her mummy
love to cook together...

and at teatime, they
talk about their day.

Hello Kitty thinks her mummy
always looks lovely...

no matter what she wears!

Mummy takes Hello Kitty
on great days out.

They love to laugh together!

When Hello Kitty
is hurt or upset...

Mummy is there to kiss it better.

Mummy gives the best tickles ever.

They make Hello Kitty
laugh and laugh!

Hello Kitty loves to watch
her mummy get dressed up...

especially when
she can help!

Mummy loves to chat on the phone...

almost as much as Hello Kitty!

Hello Kitty loves
listening to Mummy sing...

even when she gets
the words wrong!

Mummy tells the best bedtime stories.

They make Hello Kitty
feel peaceful and happy.

Hello Kitty loves her mummy very much...

and Mummy loves
Hello Kitty very much too.

How much
do you love
your mummy?

The world of
Hello Kitty

Enjoy all of these wonderful Hello Kitty books.

Picture books

Activity books

Where's Hello Kitty?

...and more!

Hello Kitty and friends story book series